Grandma and me

Rabbit

My Mom's Having a Baby!

Dori Hillestad Butler

Illustrated by
Carol Thompson

Albert Whitman & Company, Morton Grove, Illinois

For Cyndi and Ted—D.H.B.
For Jane—C.T.

Library of Congress Cataloging-in-Publication Data

Butler, Dori Hillestad.
My mom's having a baby! / by Dori Hillestad Butler ; illustrated by Carol Thompson.
p. cm.
ISBN 0-8075-5344-1 (hardcover)
1. Pregnancy—Juvenile literature. 2. Childbirth—Juvenile literature.
I. Title: My mom is having a baby! II. Thompson, Carol, ill. III. Title.
RG525.5.B88 2005   618.2—dc22   2004018585

Text copyright © 2005 by Dori Hillestad Butler.
Illustrations copyright © 2005 by Carol Thompson.
Published in 2005 by Albert Whitman & Company, 6340 Oakton Street, Morton Grove, Illinois 60053-2723.
Published simultaneously in Canada by Fitzhenry & Whiteside, Markham, Ontario.

Printed in China through Colorcraft Ltd., Hong Kong.
10 9 8 7 6 5 4 3 2 1

The art is rendered in watercolor. The design is by Carol Gildar.

For more information about Albert Whitman & Company, please visit our web site at www.albertwhitman.com.

Hi, I'm Elizabeth. This is my mom and dad. You can't tell by looking at my mom, but there's a baby growing inside her. That baby is going to be my little brother or sister.

September

We just found out about our baby, but he's been inside my mom for four weeks. He's floating in a special place inside her belly called the uterus. He doesn't look much like a baby yet, but that's because he's only as big as my bottom front tooth. He already has a head, a backbone, and buds that will grow into arms and legs. He also has a heart that's already started beating.

It's September now, but he won't be born until May. That's a long time to wait.

Real size

baby

uterus

magnified many times

October

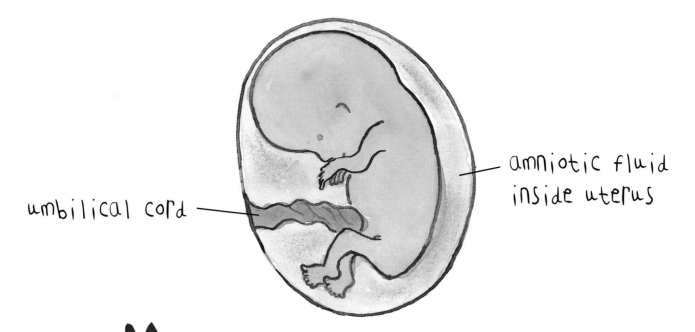

umbilical cord

amniotic fluid inside uterus

Mom's uterus is like a balloon that grows bigger and bigger. Our baby is nice and cozy in there. He's not too hot and not too cold. He's surrounded by warm water called amniotic fluid. The water protects him so he doesn't get bumped around too much.

It's October now, and our baby has eyes, ears, fingers, and toes. He can't breathe by himself yet. He gets all the oxygen he needs through a twisty tube called the umbilical cord. The oxygen travels from Mom's bloodstream into our baby.

The food my mom eats travels from her bloodstream through the umbilical cord, too. I think that's a good way to eat broccoli, but it's not a very good way to eat ice cream.

burp!!

Mom has to go to the doctor a lot to make sure both she and our baby stay healthy. Sometimes she feels sick to her stomach, but the doctor says that's normal because of all the changes in her body. Mom says she'll feel better soon.

The doctor weighs Mom and measures her belly. Then she puts a little instrument called a Doppler on her belly so we can hear our baby's heart beating. It's loud and fast. It sounds like a galloping horse!

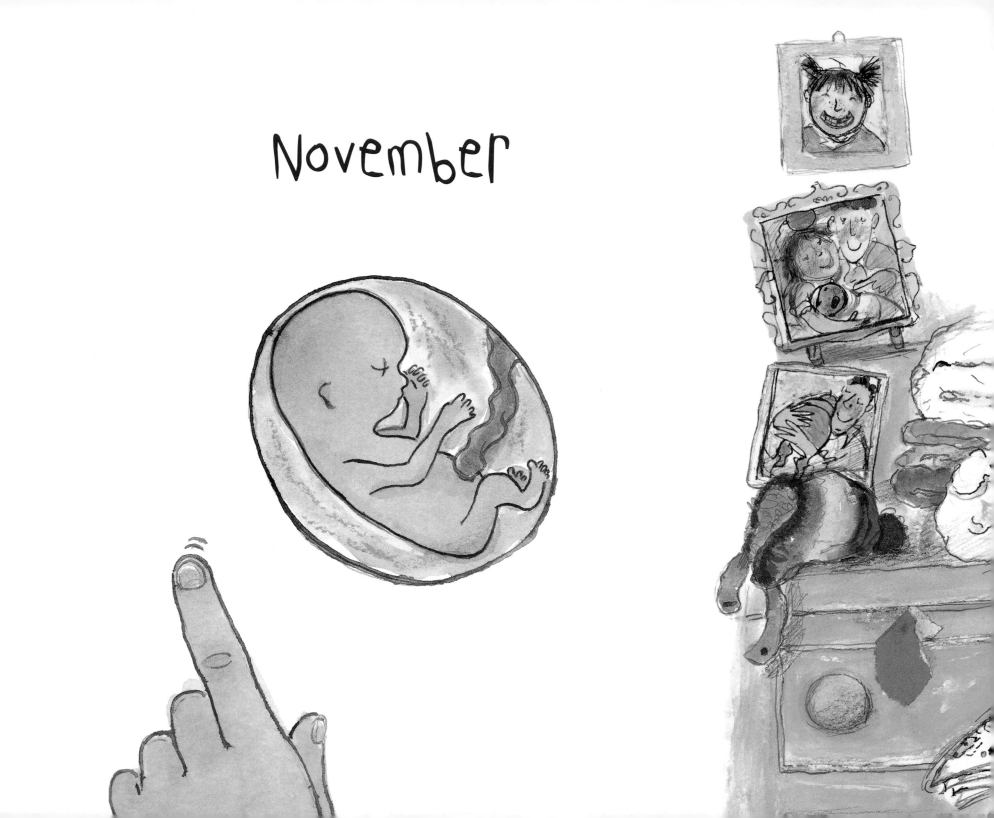

November

It's November now and our baby is twelve weeks old. All his body parts are formed, but he's only as big as my pointer finger. He has soft nails on his fingers and toes, eyelids that are shut tight, and twenty teeny, tiny buds inside his mouth that will become his teeth.

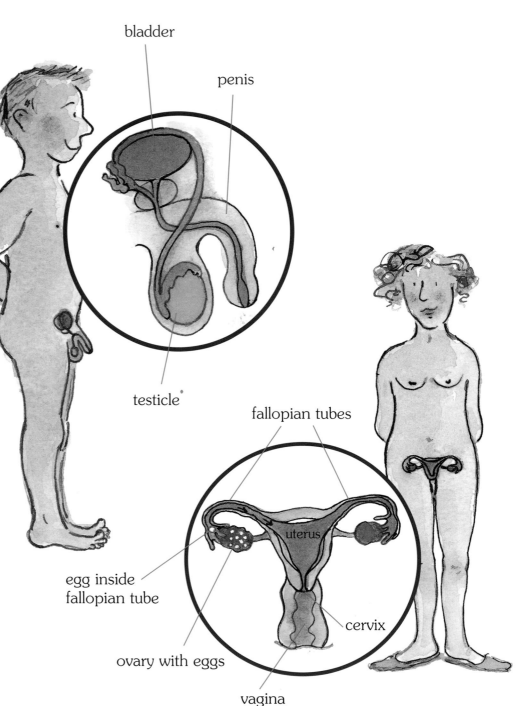

I wonder how our baby got inside my mom. One day, she and I have a nice talk about that.

Mom says it takes two people to make a baby. A man and a woman. Children can't make babies.

Tiny sperm are made inside a man's testicles. Tiny eggs are stored inside a woman's ovaries. A sperm and egg must join to make a baby.

When a sperm and egg come together, in a place called a fallopian tube, we say the egg is "fertilized." The fertilized egg moves down the fallopian tube and into the uterus. There, all snug and safe, it grows into a baby.

But how do the sperm and egg get together, I wonder?

bladder

penis

testicle

fallopian tubes

uterus

egg inside fallopian tube

cervix

ovary with eggs

vagina

Mom says that when a man and a woman love each other so much that they want to make a baby, they lie really close to each other and hug and kiss. All this hugging and kissing feels nice. It makes the man and woman want to get even closer to each other.

The man puts his penis between the woman's legs and inside her vagina. After a while, a white liquid shoots out of the man's penis and into the woman's vagina. The liquid is full of millions of sperm. They swim up the woman's vagina, through her uterus, and into one of her fallopian tubes. If a sperm and egg join together, nine months later, a new baby will be born!

Dad's sperm (like tiny tadpoles!)

Mom's egg (the actual size is like a period at the end of a sentence)

made it!

The sperm swim like mad through a fallopian tube towards Mom's egg. Only one sperm can join with the egg.

December

As long as my foot!

Our baby is growing bigger every day. Mom's belly s-t-r-e-t-c-h-e-s to make room. It's December and everyone can tell there's a baby inside her now. Her belly bulges out a little.

Our baby is about as long as my foot. He can turn sideways and backwards and upside down. Sometimes Mom can feel him turning somersaults in there.

Pretty soon I'll be able to put my hand on her belly and feel him, too. But I can't feel him yet.

January

I wonder if our baby is a boy or a girl? I hope he's a boy because we already have a girl—ME! But I don't say so out loud.

We can find out if our baby is a boy when we go to Mom's ultrasound examination. Ultrasound lets us see our baby while he's still inside my mom.

He's so cute!

Look! He's sucking his thumb!
Mom doesn't want to know whether
our baby is a boy or a girl yet. She wants to
be surprised when the baby is born.
Can't we just be surprised right now?

February

It's February now and our baby is as big as my stuffed rabbit. Guess what? He can hear! He can hear sounds inside Mom's body, like her heart beating and her stomach gurgling. He can also hear me talk and laugh and practice the piano. Sometimes, when he hears a loud noise, he jumps.

He can also open his eyes. There isn't much to see inside my mom, but he can tell the difference between light and dark.

Sometimes when I lay my hand on Mom's big, round belly, I can feel him moving. The hard bump is where his head is. I like to gently rub his head and say, "Nice baby." I think he likes it, too.

Nice baby

March and April

He's upside down!

During March and April, our baby grows bigger and stronger. He doesn't have a lot of room to turn around anymore. He settles low in Mom's uterus with his head pointed down. He's getting ready to be born.

Mom's belly is so big she can't even see her feet. She's tired a lot, and sometimes her back hurts.

May

In May, Grandma comes all the way from Florida to stay with us. She's going to take care of me when Mom and Dad go to the hospital to have our baby.

I like it when Grandma comes. We bake cookies and play dominoes and just talk things over.

Two days after Grandma arrives, Mom shouts, "My water broke!" The water that protected our baby dribbles down Mom's leg and makes a puddle on the floor.

That means our baby is coming!

Mom starts to have contractions. Contractions are pains she gets in her belly when her uterus squeezes. All that squeezing helps our baby get born.

Mom does some special breathing to help with the contractions.

Dad rushes home from work and drives Mom to the hospital.

Grandma and I wait.   And wait.   And wait . . .

It takes a long time to have a baby. First the cervix at the bottom of Mom's uterus has to open wide enough so our baby can get through. Then Mom has to push our baby down through her vagina and out between her legs.

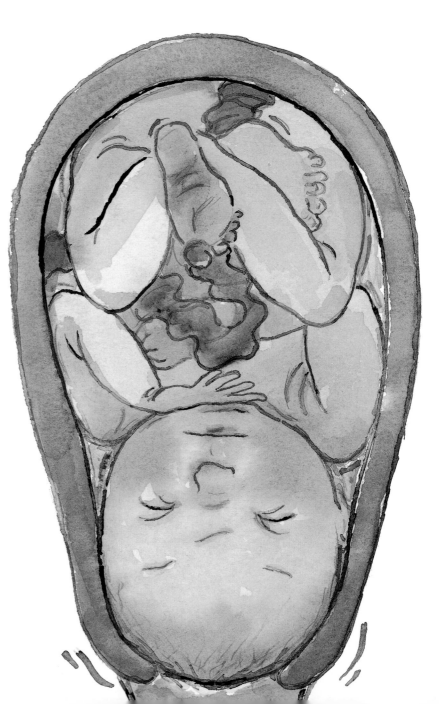

This is hard work for my mom. That's why *everyone* says she's *in labor* right now.

Finally Dad calls us on the phone. Our baby is here!

Isn't he beautiful?
He's got blue eyes and brown hair
and really chubby cheeks. The little
stump on his belly is what's left
of his umbilical cord. The doctor
says it'll fall off in a couple of
weeks. Then he'll have a
belly button, just like me.

from
**Big
Sister!**

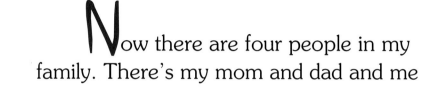

Now there are four people in my family. There's my mom and dad and me

and . . .

Hello, baby!

my little brother,

Michael.

May 19

Michael's Birthday!

My mom

Mom, Dad, and me

Me in my bassinet

Me, again